MY FANTASTIC FIELD TRIP
Junior Discovers Saving

by **Dave Ramsey**

Collect all of the *Junior's Adventures* books!

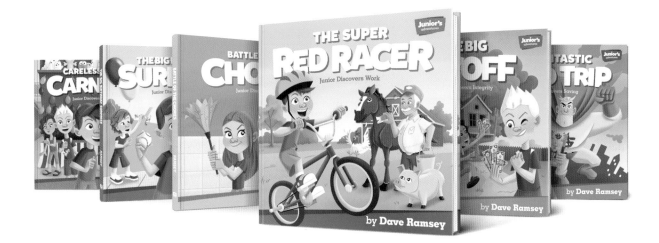

My Fantastic Field Trip: Junior Discovers Saving
© 2015 Lampo Licensing, LLC
Published by Ramsey Press, The Lampo Group, Inc.
Brentwood, TN 37027

For more information on Dave Ramsey, visit daveramsey.com or call 888.227.3223.

Editors: Amy Parker, Jen Gingerich
Project Management: Preston Cannon, Bryan Amerine and Mallory Darcy
Illustrations: Greg Hardin, John Trent and Kenny Yamada
Art Direction: Luke LeFevre, Brad Dennison and Chris Carrico

DEDICATION

To my grandchildren, William and Amelia Jane. You (and your future siblings and cousins) are my true legacy.

Listen to your parents. They are the finest young men and women I've ever known.

It's a blessing to be their dad—and your Papa Dave.

Junior had been waiting for this day for months.

Today was the day—*finally the day*—that he would meet the real Dollar Bill!

Junior squirmed in his seat while Ms. Harper called the roll.

When she finally called his name, Junior yelled, **"HERE!"**

Ms. Harper laughed. "Junior, are you excited about our field trip today?"

"Yes, Ms. Harper! *The Adventures of Dollar Bill* is my favorite show!"

On the bus, Junior checked his pocket to make sure his $20 was still in his Spend envelope. He had been saving his commission money to buy a Dollar Bill action figure.

"What do you think Dollar Bill will be like in person?" Maddie asked him.

Billy raised his arm and said in his best Dollar Bill voice, "My mission is to destroy debt, carry cash, and teach kids how to give, save, and spend responsibly."

SPEND

Junior laughed. "Just imagine what we could do if *we* were superheroes like Dollar Bill."

When they arrived at the studio, Junior was the first one in the lobby. He couldn't believe that he was finally here in the presence of a hero.

There was a gift shop to the left with shelves full of Dollar Bill action figures. To the right was a glass-walled studio where the greatest Dollar Bill adventures played out each and every week.

"Welcome, kids," a guy called from the center of the lobby. "I'm Ben, your tour guide. Thank you for visiting today! We've got exactly seven minutes and thirty-seven seconds before quiet on the set. So, everyone follow me!"

Junior's class walked down the hall until they reached a door that read Stage One.

"All right, kids. Everyone keep quiet as we step inside."

"Scene two, take one!" A man slammed the arm of a clapboard.

"Action!" the director yelled from her chair.

Tour guide Ben held a finger to his lips as they all looked out at the set in front of them. It looked like a real neighborhood!

A boy rode a bike onto the set and tossed a newspaper onto a driveway.

Just then, Dollar Bill flew into the scene.

"Good aim, Charles!" Dollar Bill said. "You sure are working hard!" The boy stopped his bike. "Hey, Dollar Bill! Yeah, I'm delivering papers to save money for a new bike!"

"Wow! How much have you saved?" Dollar Bill asked.

"I have $75 saved so far, but I still have a long way to go," Charles said, sounding a little disappointed.

"Saving takes time. But you know what? You will be so proud of yourself when you pay cash for that new bike," Dollar Bill said.

"Thank you, Dollar Bill!" Charles flashed a big smile.

"Way to be a Super Saver, Charles!" said Dollar Bill.

"Aaand cut!" A voice boomed from the set.

Immediately, the crew rushed in to change the set, and, within minutes, the set was transformed into a park complete with grass, a walking path, and a playground backdrop.

The man with the clapboard yelled, "Scene three, take one!"

"Aaaand action!" said the director.

A girl stepped onto the set, walking four small dogs—with two leashes in one hand and two in the other. One of the dogs bounced excitedly.

"Settle down, Einstein!" The girl said sternly. The dog stopped jumping and started walking next to the other dogs.

Just then, Dollar Bill flew into the scene.
"Hi, Rosie! It looks like you have your hands full!"

"Hi, Dollar Bill! Yes, I'm walking my neighbors' dogs for extra money."

"Oh, yeah? Are you saving for something special?"

"Well, my dad says maybe some day I can use the money for my very own car," Rosie answered.

"Wow!" Dollar Bill exclaimed. "Now that's what I call super saving! Your patience and hard work are sure to pay off."

Rosie beamed. "I hope so, Dollar Bill!"

"Aand cut! Take five," the director shouted.

As the crew began changing the set again, Junior looked through the glass wall of the studio, past the lobby, and into the gift shop. He saw the Dollar Bill action figures on the shelves and checked his pocket again for his Spend envelope.

"All right, kids," Ben said, "This will be the last scene for today. Then you'll get to meet Dollar Bill!"

The kids got quiet. The set had changed once more, but this time it was the same set that closed every single *The Adventures of Dollar Bill* show: Life Lessons with Dollar Bill.

Dollar Bill was standing in the center of the stage facing the camera.

"Scene five, take one!" said the man with the clapboard. "And action!" yelled the director.

"Hello, kids!" Dollar Bill spoke to the camera.

"Today, we saw two super kids, Charles and Rosie, who were working hard to save. They are learning that saving takes hard work, patience, and time.

"And while there's nothing wrong with spending money that you worked hard for, saving is important too. In fact, it takes superhero strength!

"Can you think of something you'd like to save your money for? Maybe a toy, a car, or even college? You can be a Super Saver just like Charles or Rosie. It's hard work, but it's so worth it!"

"Aaand cut! That's a wrap!" said the director, standing from her chair.

Junior had butterflies in his stomach as he watched Dollar Bill walk toward his class.

"Hey, kids!" Dollar Bill smiled. "Did you like today's show?"

"Yes!" Junior's class exclaimed together.

"Excellent!" said Dollar Bill.
"It sounds like you all are on
your way to becoming Super
Savers too! Well, I had better be off!
Even superheroes have to eat lunch."
And with that, Dollar Bill
dashed away.

In the gift shop, Junior held his $20 and pulled a Dollar Bill action figure off the shelf. He looked at his money and imagined what he could do with it if he saved it.

Junior returned the action figure to the shelf. Then, he placed his money back in his Spend envelope. When he got home that afternoon, he would move the money back to his Save envelope.

The Dollar Bill action figure
could wait until another day.
Today, Junior wanted to be a
Super Saver.

As Junior took his seat on the bus, he felt proud of himself. He felt like a real superhero! He knew that this was one field trip he'd never forget.